# PROFESSOR CLARK

## THE SCIENCE SHARK®

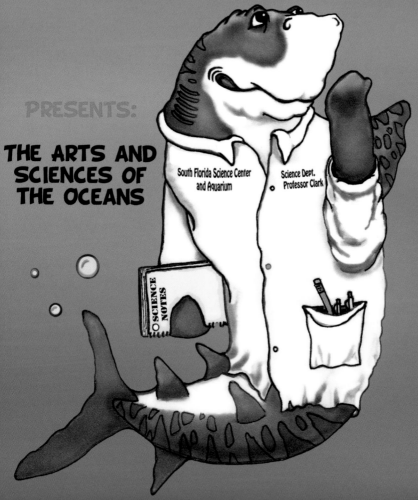

PRESENTS:

THE ARTS AND
SCIENCES OF
THE OCEANS

WWW.PROFESSORCLARKTHESCIENCESHARK.COM

*PROFESSOR CLARK THE SCIENCE SHARK Book 4 **Reada's Rescue**™*
™Trademark Reg. No. 4,450,531
Copyright © 2015 by Scott and Karen Lamberson.
All rights reserved.

Published by Professor Clark the Science Shark
2433 Hope Lane
Palm Beach Gardens, FL 33410
www.ProfessorClarktheScienceShark.com

Book layout by SuOakes Graphic Design, Lake Worth, FL
www.suoakesdesign.com

Printed in the United States by Jostens in Clarksville, TN
ISBN: 978-1-5136-0188-5

Greetings from the sea, land lovers!

I'm Professor Clark the Science Shark, and I'd like to tell you about my delightful and educational book series starring me, of course. In this book, Book 4: *Reada's Rescue*, my human friend, Andrew, and I meet Reada, a beautiful and endangered Hawksbill turtle that really needs our help!

Together, along with Ray the Remora and Holt the Seahorse, our aquatic journeys are shared with numerous other sea creatures that want to help us in our quest to save our seas!

Much has changed in my life since I was just a young shark pup in "Book 1: *The Beginning*". That's when I met Andrew, a small red-haired boy who loved to fish and explore the ocean! Even after he swam away, I couldn't seem to get that boy out of my mind. Then I met Ray the Remora, who became my constant companion, and shares my quest to save our oceans! In Book 2: *Going Home*, I have grown up considerably and Ray gives me my full name after I prove to be incredibly knowledgeable about the science aspects of the oceans. I felt a strong need to head back home to my birthplace. When I got to Jupiter and saw the condition of the reef I knew why I had come home. I had to help! By Book 3, *The Encounter* Andrew the boy has become a man, and I am a full grown tiger shark. We finally meet up again and our bond is strengthened after I give Andrew the gift of a lifetime! We both somehow know that this is truly just the beginning of our unusual but beautiful friendship!

Fincerly,

*Professor Clark The Science Shark*

Make sure you visit us at our educational
website and social media!

www.ProfessorClarktheScienceShark.com
Instagram: @professorclarkthescienceshark
Facebook: https://www.facebook.com/ProfessorClark

4

It was a humid and hazy summer morning, and a beautiful Hawksbill turtle was swimming slowly. Her jeweled body slipped silently through the *tropical* turquoise waters of the Gulfstream several miles east of the Jupiter, Florida coastline.

As the Hawksbill swam, she passed a vast assortment of tropical fish, **crustaceans** and a variety of other sea creatures. The turtle even swam right by her favorite food, a sea sponge. She was so distracted that she didn't even notice she was being followed...by a seahorse.

That brightly colored, **curious** seahorse was named Holt, and he wanted to **investigate** why the turtle was swimming so slowly. She seemed to be exhausted and was breathing heavily with labored breaths. Her patterned body also kept bobbing to the ocean surface. Holt determined something had to be terribly wrong with the **endangered** Hawksbill turtle!

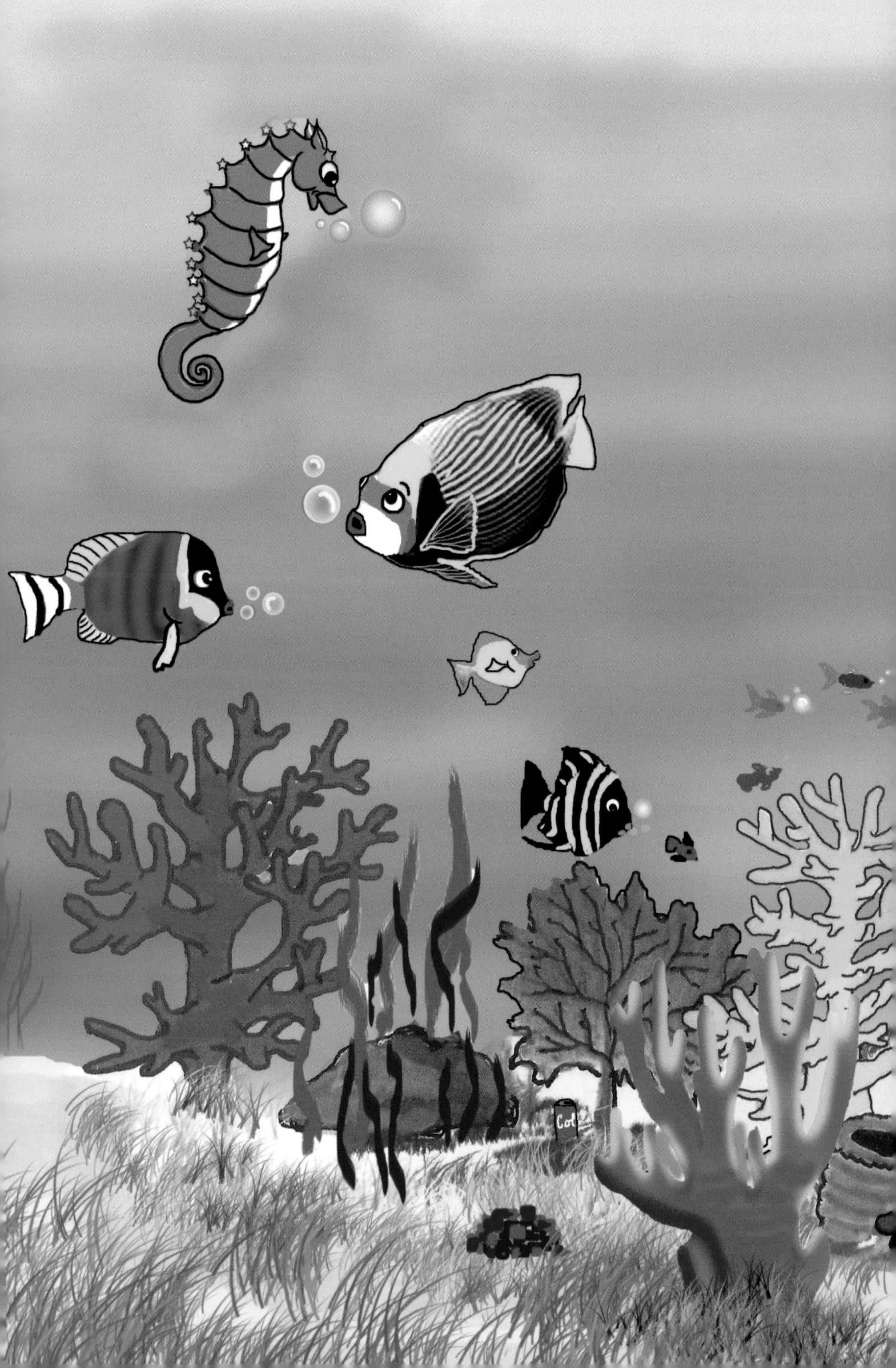

Holt concluded from her **behavior** that the **magnificent** turtle was most likely ill, perhaps from something she ate. Holt also knew that he would have to get her help, so he went to find the best help possible, Professor Clark the Science Shark!

Holt didn't have to search for Professor Clark very long. He found him and his sidekick, Ray the Remora, nearby on Hope Reef. Both Professor Clark and Ray were visibly upset as they pointed to the trash and **marine debris** on their cherished reef.

"I don't understand how somebody can be so careless. I don't understand it at all!" Ray declared with dismay. Professor Clark was also sad and concerned that their beautiful reef was indeed littered with marine debris and covered with algae!

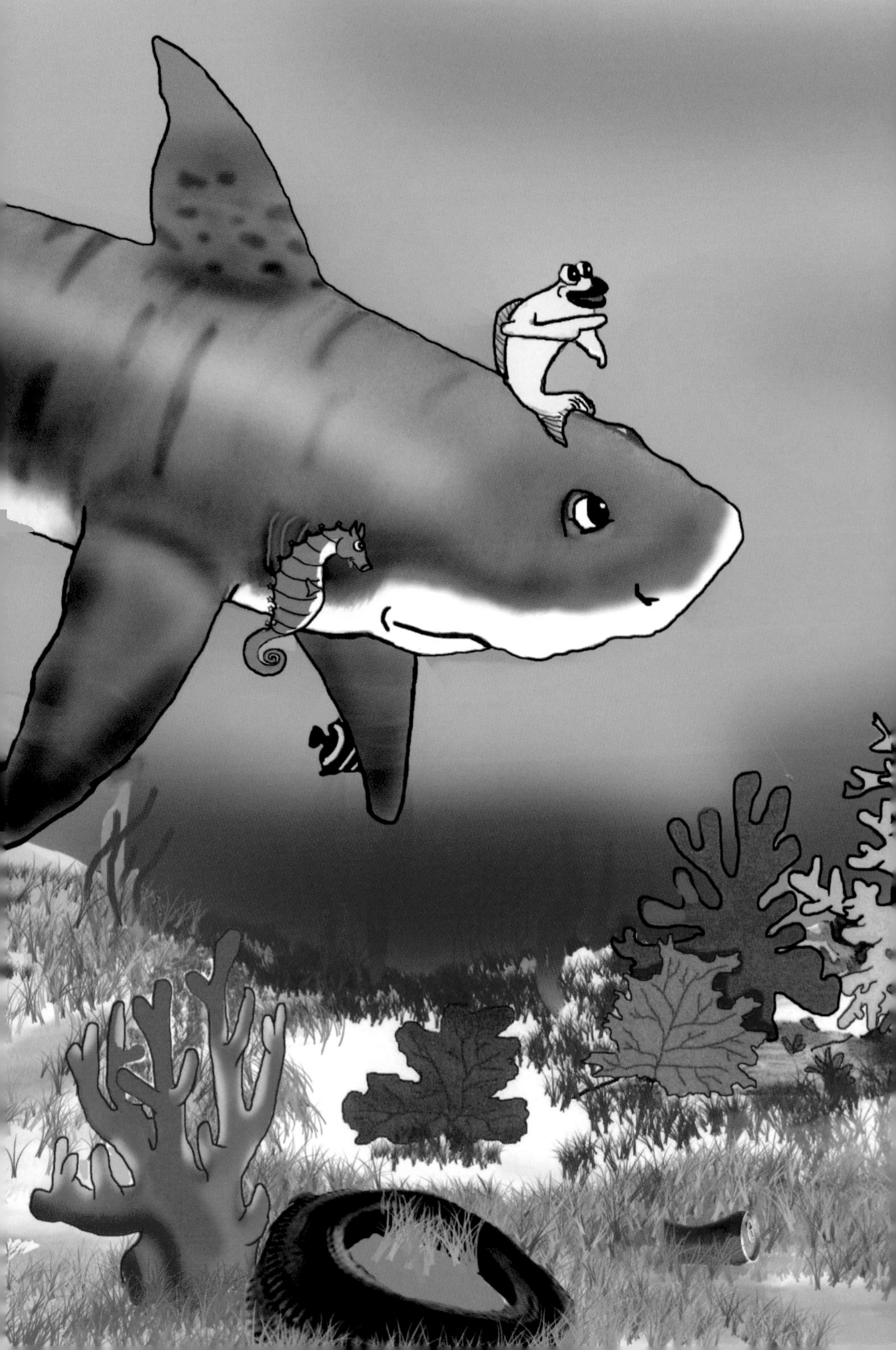

Holt knew that it was time to tell Professor Clark about the ailing Hawksbill turtle, and he spoke with **urgency**, "There is a sick sea turtle that needs our help. Please, we must hurry!" Ray and Holt clung to Professor Clark's head and the three friends searched until they saw the struggling turtle ahead.

The poor turtle was swimming slowly, but stopped to look at the approaching trio with a look of **desperation** and fear in her eyes. She tried to lift her head, but she was too weak. "Please don't be afraid," Professor Clark said with compassion. "I'm Professor Clark the Science Shark and this is Holt the Seahorse and Ray the Remora. They are my friends. We are here to help you in any way we can! I promise!"

The sick turtle replied in a **weak** voice, almost a **whisper**, "My name is Reada and I can't really describe what's wrong with me. I'm having a difficult time eating because I don't have an **appetite**. I feel really sick! Right now all I want to do is sleep and float to the water's surface. I know that's not right."

Professor Clark the Science Shark knew he had to act quickly if his attempts to save Reada would be successful.

So the concerned Professor Clark and his friends began desperately searching for some healthy **sea sponges** hoping to **nourish** the sickened turtle. But they knew they would need more than just food to save Reada.

While he was looking for sea sponges, Professor Clark saw something very familiar to him. It was the special cherished lure that belonged to his human friend Andrew! Professor Clark knew how Andrew loved to fish, so Andrew had to be close by! Suddenly the lure started moving, so Professor Clark followed it. He followed the lure all the way to Andrew's boat.

Andrew just happened to be in his boat fishing on Hope Reef, and while he was hoping to catch something to bring home, he couldn't help but think about his friend Professor Clark. Every time he fished on his favorite reef, he daydreamed about swimming with that shark again.

As he was reeling in his fishing line, he couldn't help but see the shadowy figure in the water below! Could it be? Andrew couldn't believe his eyes! It certainly looked like his favorite tiger shark, Professor Clark the Science Shark!

Andrew acted quickly. He grabbed his snorkel and mask, and dove into the **aquatic oasis**, right beside his favorite shark! Professor Clark recognized Andrew right away, and coaxed the young man to follow him in hopes of rescuing Reada.

Andrew let his tiger shark friend take the lead as they descended to the troubled coral reef.

Andrew was overwhelmed with despair and concern when he saw all of the trash, litter and algae on his favorite fishing spot. It seemed to be everywhere.

As Andrew was thinking about possible plans and solutions to help restore Hope Reef, he noticed, out of the corner of his eye, the sick and weakened Hawksbill turtle in the distance, trying to stay afloat. "I'm sure this is the reason why Professor Clark wanted me to follow him," Andrew thought to himself. Andrew knew instantly he would have to swim back to his boat and call for help!

Back on his boat, Andrew immediately called The
Florida Fish and Wildlife Conservation Commission
about the sick Hawksbill turtle. They assured
Andrew that help would soon be coming from
Loggerhead Marinelife Center in
Juno Beach.

FL 2014 AH

Reada's health continued to decline, so Professor Clark, Ray and Holt stayed by her side until Andrew returned. "Reada, this is Andrew, my kind human friend. He is here to help you," Professor Clark told Reada with encouragement. Andrew paused for only a split second and then started gently lifting the weakened turtle onto his knees. He felt her gasp and tremble. Andrew reassured Reada that no harm would come to her. "Stay quiet and try to relax. It's going to be all right, I have you," Andrew whispered to her compassionately.

It wasn't long before Andrew could see the approaching rescue boat in the distance, and he waved his hands to signal his location. He tried to keep Reada steady, while he held on to her **slippery** shell. As soon as the rescue boat stopped, a very kind and impressive

33

LOGGE

rescue team of **scientists** took over and relieved Andrew of all of his responsibilities concerning the turtle. The scientists loaded Reada onto the boat and thanked Andrew for everything he had done.

While Andrew swam back to his boat, he started thinking of plans to restore Hope Reef to its original **splendor**. Andrew loved to fish and dive, and he had noticed a steady decline in the number of fish and sea creatures that he saw on his favorite reef. He accepted the fact that human carelessness had littered the reef, but was this **pollution** also affecting the health of the reef?

With all of these concerns on his mind, Andrew knew that he would return the next day with family and friends to help clean up Hope Reef. Andrew knew that no matter what, he had to be successful!

Early the next morning Andrew returned to Hope
Reef. His family and friends were saddened to see
the **enormous** amount of marine debris and algae,
but their concerns quickly turned to enthusiasm.
Everyone went right to work putting pound after
pound of trash into mesh bags. They filled bag
after bag with all kinds of plastics, glass bottles,
aluminum cans and containers, old fishing lines,
anchors, ropes and other human debris.

Everyone was careful not to disturb the delicate coral as they worked. They made sure that all of the fishing line was cut away from the fragile **ocean** coral and the beautiful sea fans. The volunteers worked all day long, until the reef once again looked pristine and vibrant!

Everybody was exhausted, but they were exhilarated! Andrew suggested that his family and friends should relax and hang out in the water with Professor Clark for a while, so that is just what they did!

A couple of **considerate** and extremely dedicated volunteers from Loggerhead Marinelife Center sorted the aluminum cans, glass and plastics in **recyclable** bags.

Weeks went by and Andrew swam with Professor Clark, Ray, and Holt on Hope Reef whenever he could. Everyone enjoyed swimming in the reef's cleaner and healthier **environment**, but they were saddened by Reada's absence. One sunny day, when Andrew was swimming with his friends on the reef, Ray noticed something slowly approaching them!

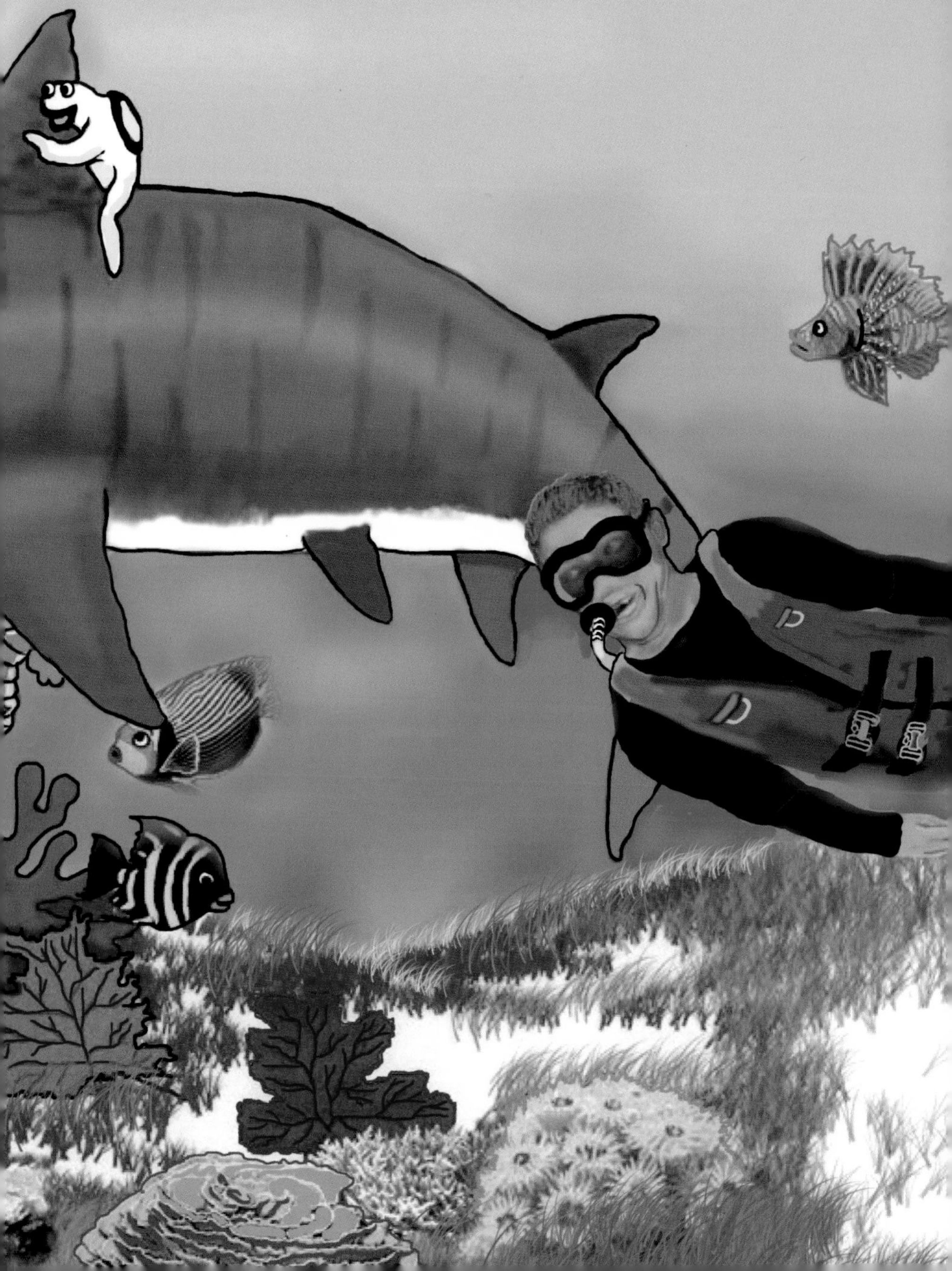

A few moments later they all saw it was Reada!
She glided over the coral reef, through the
beautiful blue water. Reada was gleaming and
looked fantastic!

"Reada!" they all cried out, "We can't believe it's really you!". Professor Clark shouted, "Andrew's family and friends cleaned up Hope Reef, so you won't get sick again! Please stay and make this your **permanent** home! We can't wait to hear all about your stay at Loggerhead Marinelife Center!"

Reada told them about her exciting journey to Loggerhead Marinelife Center in Juno Beach, Florida. "The human doctors and staff were so wonderful! They gave me several tests, and some medicine that helped me feel better right away. They gave me delicious food that helped me regain my strength. They took excellent care of me and today they decided I was healthy enough to be released back into the ocean! There was even a crowd of volunteers that cheered as I swam away!"

LOGGERHEAD
MARINELIFE CENTER

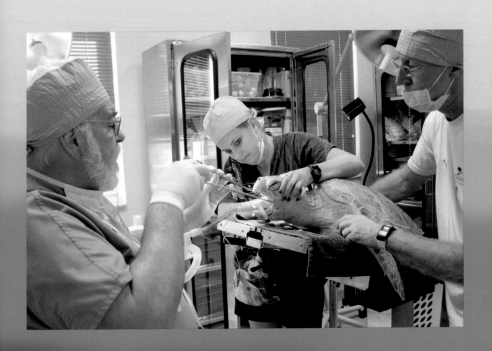

Reada was feeling healthy and **confident**. She looked at her new home and her friends and proclaimed with **admiration**, "I am delighted and humbled to be here today, and I want to thank all of you for rescuing me! You, Holt, for finding me, and Professor Clark and Ray, for finding Andrew, and Andrew, you truly saved my life!"

Andrew looked at all of them, and although he couldn't understand their animal language, he knew that they were feeling joy in their hearts.

Reada had found a new home on Hope Reef, with great new friends, who would be her friends, FOREVER!

# PROFESSOR CLARK THE SCIENCE SHARK'S VOCAB LAB

**ADMIRATION:** something regarded as impressive or worthy of respect.

**APPETITE:** the desire to eat food, sometimes due to hunger.

**AQUATIC OASIS:** pertaining to water, something serving as a refuge, a pleasant change.

**BEHAVIOR:** the way one acts or conducts oneself, especially toward others.

**CONSIDERATE:** showing careful thought, caring.

**CONFIDENT:** sure of oneself; having no uncertainty about one's own abilities.

**CRUSTACEANS:** an arthropod of the large, mainly aquatic group Crustacea, such as a crab, lobster, shrimp, or barnacle. They have a hard shell, segmented body and jointed legs.

**CURIOUS:** eager to know or learn something.

**DESPERATION:** a state of despair, typically one that results in rash or extreme behavior.

**ENDANGERED:** (of a species) seriously at risk of extinction.

**ENORMOUS:** very large in size, quantity, or extent.

**ENVIRONMENT:** the surroundings or conditions in which a person, animal, or plant lives or operates.

**IMMENSE:** extremely large or great, huge, massive.

**INVESTIGATE:** carry out research or study so as to discover facts or information.

**MAGNIFICENT:** impressively beautiful, elaborate, or extravagant; striking; very good; excellent.

**MARINE DEBRIS:** any trash that makes its way into the oceans.

**NOURISH:** provide with the food or other substances necessary for growth, health, and good condition.

**OCEAN:** the vast body of salt water that covers almost 3/4ths of the earth's surface. There are 5 oceans, the Atlantic, Pacific, Indian, Arctic, and Antarctic.

**PERMANENT:** lasting or intended to last or remain unchanged indefinitely.

**POLLUTION:** the presence in or introduction into the environment of a substance or thing that has harmful or poisonous effects.

**RECYCLABLE:** treated or processed to make suitable for reuse.

**SCIENTISTS:** individuals who are studying or have expert knowledge of one or more of the natural or physical sciences.

**SEA SPONGES:** any number of numerous aquatic, chiefly marine feeding invertebrate animals characteristically having a porous skeleton composed of fibrous material often forming colonies attached to underwater surfaces.

**SLIPPERY:** difficult to hold firmly or stand on because it is smooth, wet, or slimy.

**SPLENDOR:** brilliant or gorgeous appearance, coloring, etc.

**TROPICAL:** a warm to hot region or climate with plenty of precipitation year-round.

**URGENCY:** importance requiring swift action

**WHISPER:** to speak very softly using one's breath without one's vocal cords, especially for the sake of privacy.

# PROFESSOR CLARK'S FUN FIN FACTS

## ▶ Remora Fish

Ray the Remora is a remora fish. Remora fish are sometimes called sucker fish. This is because their dorsal fin is an oval sucker that can help them attach to other marine animals. The marine animal to which the remora attaches is called the host animal. The remora and its host animal have a symbiotic (sim-bee-AH-tik) relationship. This means both animals benefit each other.

In the case of Professor Clark the Science Shark and Ray the Remora, Professor Clark provides protection and food for Ray. Ray eats dead skin and parasites on Professor Clark to keep him clean and healthy.

Research: What other animals have a symbiotic relationship? Describe their relationship.

## ▶ Hawksbill Turtle

Hawksbills are named for their narrow, pointed beak. They also have a distinctive pattern of overlapping scales on their shells that form a serrated-look on the edges. These colored and patterned shells are highly valuable and are commonly sold as "tortoise shell" in markets. Hawksbills are found throughout the world's tropical oceans, predominantly in coral/coastal reefs. They feed mainly on sponges by using their narrow pointed beaks to extract them from crevices on the reef, but also eat sea anemones and jellyfish.

Sea turtles are the living representatives of a group of reptiles that has existed on Earth and traveled our seas for the last 150 million years. They are a fundamental link in marine ecosystems and help maintain the health of coral reefs and sea grass beds.

Research: What is the main threat to the endangered Hawksbill turtles and why?

▶ Coral Reef

There are three major types of reefs around the world. These include fringe reefs, barrier reefs, and atolls. Fringe reefs grow near the shore. Barrier reefs grow farther away from the shore and have a lagoon between the reef and the shore. Atolls grow around the rim of an extinct volcano. The Florida Reef Tract runs from the Florida Keys to the St. Lucie Inlet. Florida's coral reefs are most similar to barrier reefs, but do not have the lagoons. Florida also has patch reefs, which are smaller and grow between the reef tract and the shore in the shallow waters. Hope Reef is a patch reef.

Research: What is the name of the largest coral reef in the world? Where is it?

## ▶ Loggerhead Marinelife Center

Nestled along Florida's Atlantic coast in Juno Beach, Florida, Loggerhead Marinelife Center (LMC) has protected Florida's coastal ecosystems and provided ocean conservation education to children, families, and visitors for over 30 years. The nonprofit facility offers free admission and educates over 300,000 visitors annually on their continued mission: to promote conservation of Florida's coastal ecosystems with a special focus on threatened and endangered sea turtles.

The center is adjacent to one of the most densely nested loggerhead sea turtle beaches in the world, providing staff biologists with 9.5 miles of beach to monitor and further research the precious and endangered sea turtle. Sea turtle nesting season runs from March 1 to October 31 on Florida's Atlantic Coast. Three species of sea turtles nest on local beaches – loggerhead, leatherback and green sea turtles. For more information, visit www.marinelife.org and stay connected with them via Facebook, Twitter and Instagram.

**Research: What is one of the biggest dangers to hatchlings?**

## Swimming through Standards

SC.2.N.1.1 Raise questions about the natural world, investigate them in teams through free exploration and systematic observations, and generate appropriate explanations based on those explorations.

SC.2.N.1.3 Ask, "how do you know?" in appropriate situations and attempt reasonable answers when asked the same question by others.

SC.2.N.1.5 Distinguish between empirical observation (what you see, hear, feel, smell, or taste) and ideas or inferences (what you think).

SC.2.N.1.6 Explain how scientists alone or in groups are always investigating new ways to solve problems.

SC.2.L.17.1 Compare and contrast the basic needs that all living things, including humans, have for survival.

SC.2.L.17.2 Recognize and explain that living things are found all over Earth, but each is only able to live in habitats that meet its basic needs.

SC.3.N.1.1 Raise questions about the natural world, investigate them individually and in teams through free exploration and systematic investigations, and generate appropriate explanations based on those explorations. (Assessed as SC.5.N.1.1)

SC.3.N.1.4 Recognize the importance of communication among scientists

SC.3.N.1.7 Explain that empirical evidence is information, such as observations or measurements that is used to help validate explanations of natural phenomena. (Assessed as SC.5.N.2.1)

SC.4.N.1.1 Raise questions about the natural world, use appropriate reference materials that support understanding to obtain information (identifying the source), conduct both individual and team investigations through free exploration and systematic investigations. (Assessed as SC.5.N.1.1)

SC.4.N.1.2 Compare the observations made by different groups using multiple tools and seek reasons to explain the differences across groups. (Assessed as SC.5.N.2.2)

SC.4.N.1.3 Explain that science does not always follow a rigidly defined method ("the scientific method") but that science does involve the use of observations and empirical evidence. (Assessed as SC.5.N.2.1)

SC.4.N.1.6 Keep records that describe observations made, carefully distinguishing actual observations from ideas and inferences about the observations. (Assessed as SC.5.N.1.1)

SC.4.N.1.7 Recognize and explain that scientists base their explanations on evidence. (Assessed as SC.5.N.2.1)

SC.4.N.2.1 Explain that science focuses solely on the natural world.

SC.4.L.17.2 Explain that animals, including humans, cannot make their own food and that when animals eat plants or other animals, the energy stored in the food source is passed to them. (Assessed as SC.4.L.17.3)

SC.4.L.17.4 Recognize ways plants and animals, including humans, can affect the environment. (Assessed as SC.5.L.17.1)

SC.5.N.1.2 Explain the difference between an experiment and other types of scientific investigation.　　(Assessed as SC.5.N.1.1)

SC.5.N.1.5 Recognize and explain that authentic scientific investigation frequently does not parallel the steps of "scientific method." (Assessed as SC.5.N.2.1)

SC.5.N.1.6 Recognize and explain the difference between personal opinion/interpretation and verified observation. (Assessed as SC.5.N.2.1)

SC.5.N.2.1 Recognize and explain that science is grounded in empirical observations that are testable; explanation must always be linked with evidence. Also assessed: SC.3.N.1.7, SC.4.N.1.3, SC.4.N.1.7, SC.5.N.1.5, SC.5.N.1.6

SC.5.L.17.1 Compare and contrast adaptations displayed by animals and plants that enable them to survive in different environments such as life cycles variations, animal behaviors and physical characteristics. Also assessed: SC.3.L.17.1, SC.4.L.16.2, SC.4.L.16.3, SC.4.L.17.1, SC.4.L.17.4, SC.5.L.15.1

SC.5.L.15.1 Describe how, when the environment changes, differences between individuals allow some plants and animals to survive and reproduce while others die or move to new locations. (Assessed as SC.5.L.17.1)

# Andrew "Red" Harris Foundation

Lobsters like to hide in the cones on our snorkel trail modules and in the open spaces at the bottom.

There are beautiful tropical fish like these blue and french angelfish, butterfly fish, wrasses, tophats, coral shrimp and even seahorses on the Blue Heron Bridge snorkel trail, but you have to get up close to really see them!

This green moray likes module 10 on the snorkel trail.

That's Martha holding her breath and looking inside one of our coral head modules.

A pair of goliath groupers sharing a pyramid module on one of our offshore reefs.

Do you see the goliath grouper in the middle of the small fish? Why are the small fish following it?

*http://AndrewRedHarrisFoundation.org 18230 River Oaks Dr., Jupiter, Fl 33458*